Clifford THE BIG RED DOG®

Scholastic

Fishing Lessons

Adapted by Alison Inches
From the television script "Fishing Lessons" by Bob Carrau
Illustrated by Jose Maria Cardona

Based on the Scholastic book series
"Clifford The Big Red Dog" by Norman Bridwell

ISBN 0-439-45809-9

15 14 13 12 11 10   10 11 12 13 140

Design by Peter Koblish

Printed in the U.S.A.   40

First printing, March 2003

SCHOLASTIC INC.

New York   Toronto   London   Auckland   Sydney
Mexico City   New Delhi   Hong Kong   Buenos Aires

"I've got a bite!" cried Charley as he reeled in a big fish.
"Wow!" said Emily Elizabeth. "I wish I knew how to fish."
"I could teach you tomorrow," said Charley.
"Great!" Emily Elizabeth replied.

The next morning, Emily Elizabeth raced down the pier for her fishing lesson.
But Charley was checking out Vaz's new model airplane.
"Let's go to the park and fly it!" said Charley. "We'll fish tomorrow, Emily Elizabeth! *Come on!*"

Everyone took turns flying the plane . . .

even Clifford!

The next day, Charley wanted to play on the new rope swing at the lagoon.
"We'll fish tomorrow, Emily Elizabeth," said Charley.
"Well, okay," said Emily Elizabeth.
"Look out below!" cried Charley.

The following day, Emily Elizabeth waited at the pier, but Charley never showed up.
"He must have forgotten about us," said Emily Elizabeth.

"We'll just have to teach ourselves how to fish."
Clifford barked approvingly.

It took them a few tries to get the hang of it.

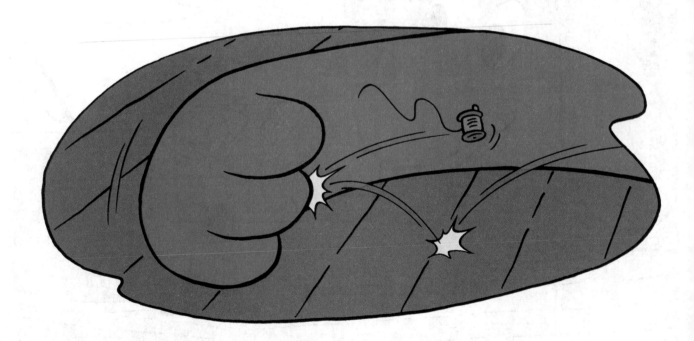

Finally, Emily Elizabeth cast the line over the water.

Then she hopped onto Clifford's front paw and waited for the fish to bite.

At the lagoon, Charley played on the rope swing again. "Wahooo!"

"I knew you'd be here, Charley," Jetta said, with her hands on her hips.

"What do you mean?" said Charley.

"You promised to teach Emily Elizabeth how to fish," said Jetta, "and now she's trying to teach herself."

Charley felt terrible.

"I hope it's not too late to fix things," he said.

Charley ran all the way to the pier.
"Hi, Emily Elizabeth," he said. "Catch anything?"
"Nope," she said.
"Eat any worms?" he asked.
"Nope."
"I'm sorry I didn't keep my promise," he said.
"Would you like some help now?"

Emily Elizabeth stared at the water.
Her line gave a little lurch.

Then her line tugged taut.
"Yes!" said Emily Elizabeth. "I'd like some help right now!
I just got a bite and it's a BIG one!"
They pulled and pulled.

Clifford helped.
SNAP! The line broke and they tumbled onto
the pier in a heap.

"That doesn't matter," said Charley. "*Every* fisherman has to have a story about the 'big one' that got away."

"Wow," said Charley. "Now you're an official fisherman!"
Emily Elizabeth looked surprised.
"But I didn't catch anything!" she said.